Wake Up, Big Red Chicken!

Adapted by **GABRIELLE REYES**

SCHOLASTIC INC.

© 2025 Viacom International Inc. All Rights Reserved. Nickelodeon, Dora and all related titles, logos and characters are trademarks of Viacom International Inc.

All rights reserved. Published by Scholastic Inc., *Publishers since 1920.* SCHOLASTIC and associated logos are trademarks and/or registered trademarks of Scholastic Inc.

The publisher does not have any control over and does not assume any responsibility for author or third-party websites or their content.

No part of this publication may be reproduced, stored in a retrieval system, or transmitted in any form or by any means, electronic, mechanical, photocopying, recording, or otherwise, or used to train any artificial intelligence technologies, without written permission of the publisher. For information regarding permission, write to Scholastic Inc., Attention: Permissions Department, 557 Broadway, New York, NY 10012.

This book is a work of fiction. Names, characters, places, and incidents are either the product of the author's imagination or are used fictitiously, and any resemblance to actual persons, living or dead, business establishments, events, or locales is entirely coincidental.

ISBN 978-1-5461-2016-2

10 9 8 7 6 5 4 3 2 1   25 26 27 28 29

Printed in the U.S.A.   40

First printing 2025

Book interior design by Two Red Shoes Design

It was a sunny day.

Dora and Boots wanted to swim.

They wanted to float with the Big Red Chicken.

But where was he?

Big Red Chicken was big and red.

He was not hard to find.

But Big Red Chicken was sleeping.
He was floating away!

Where was he going?

Dora and Boots asked Map.

Map found Big Red Chicken.

He was floating toward a big waterfall!

Dora and Boots ran to catch up.

They needed to wake up Big Red Chicken!

Dora and Boots saw a Tickle Fish.

They asked for the fish's help waking up Big Red Chicken.

Tickle Fish swam to the snoring Big Red Chicken.

She tickled his feet.

She tickled his wing.

She tickled his beak.

But Big Red Chicken did not wake up.

Instead, Big Red Chicken grabbed the Tickle Fish.

He used the Tickle Fish as a pillow!

Big Red Chicken floated farther away.
Dora and Boots ran to catch up.

Just then, they heard Swiper the Fox!

Swiper tried to swipe Boots's floaty.

Boots said, "Swiper, no swiping!"

Dora said it, too. "Swiper, no swiping!"

They said it together. "Swiper, no swiping!"

Swiper fell into the river.

The Tickle Fish tickled him!

"Ohhh maaan!" Swiper said.

Boots was happy his floaty was safe.

Now it was time to wake up Big Red Chicken!

Big Red Chicken was far down the river.

Dora and Boots needed to catch up fast.

They asked Tico for help.

Tico's boat was very fast!

Dora and Boots climbed into Tico's boat.

They set out on their way!

Farther down the river, there were two paths.

Which way should they go?

"There is Big Red Chicken!" Dora said.

They followed the path lined with blue rocks.

Dora, Boots, and Tico sped up to catch him.

They got close to Big Red Chicken.

They called out, "Wake up, Big Red Chicken!"

Big Red Chicken woke up!

"*Bawk, bawk!* Where am I?" he asked.

Boots yelled to Big Red Chicken to watch out for the waterfall.

Big Red Chicken jumped onto the shore just in time.

"Thanks for waking me up!" he said.

Dora and Boots cheered. "We did it!"

Now everyone could float.
Together, they made a big splash!